Boston (Mass.) City Council

Proceedings of the City Council of Boston, April 17, 1865

on occasion of the death of Abraham Lincoln, President of the United

States

Boston (Mass.) City Council

Proceedings of the City Council of Boston, April 17, 1865
on occasion of the death of Abraham Lincoln, President of the United States

ISBN/EAN: 9783337401184

Printed in Europe, USA, Canada, Australia, Japan

Cover: Foto ©Andreas Hilbeck / pixelio.de

More available books at **www.hansebooks.com**

PROCEEDINGS

OF THE

CITY COUNCIL OF BOSTON,

APRIL 17, 1865,

ON OCCASION OF THE DEATH

OF

ABRAHAM LINCOLN,

PRESIDENT OF THE UNITED STATES.

BOSTON:
PUBLISHED BY ORDER OF THE CITY COUNCIL.
1865.

Printed by

J. E. FARWELL & COMPANY,

37 Congress Street, Boston.

CITY OF BOSTON.

April 17, 1865.

A SPECIAL meeting of the City Council of Boston was convened at twelve o'clock this day, by order of His Honor, Frederic W. Lincoln, Jr., Mayor, for the purpose of expressing their respect to the memory of Abraham Lincoln, the late President of the United States.

PROCEEDINGS OF THE BOARD OF ALDERMEN.

There were present at this meeting the Mayor and all the Aldermen.

The Board having been called to order by the Mayor, he spoke as follows : —

To THE HONORABLE THE CITY COUNCIL : —

GENTLEMEN : Abraham Lincoln, the President of the United States, expired at Washington on the morning of April 15, between the hours of seven and eight o'clock. The death of one so

distinguished, whose eminent services for the last four years have been so valuable to his country, and whose individual opinions and actions were considered so vital to its future welfare, has filled the nation's heart with gloom. In the midst of the jubilant and excited feelings of a grateful people, bound to him with dearer ties than ever before in his career, his connection with them has been suddenly severed by the violent hands of an assassin. The fresh joy of the recent glorious victories of our armies, securing, we trusted, peace and prosperity to a reunited country, has unexpectedly been turned to mourning.

The shouts of an exultant people are hushed, and the stern discipline of sorrow is once more to test their character and to prove their manhood. Called to the Chief Magistracy of the nation at a time of unexampled trial, when the Union of

our fathers was threatened with disruption by degenerate sons, the loyal spirit of the country responded time and time again to his patriotic appeals. His talents and his practical virtues seemed to develop and strengthen with the new exigencies which called for their exercise; and at the moment when success was crowning our efforts the great leader was summoned away, and his office and its great trusts fall upon another.

President Lincoln's career will ever be considered as one of the best illustrations of the character and nature of Republican institutions. He was emphatically a man of the people. Born in an humble condition, he was never tempted to rise by a sordid ambition for place; but yet he was ever ready to meet public responsibilities, when the country demanded his services. His merits as a statesman and patriot

have been tested in the most momentous period in the history of the Republic. His integrity and worth as a man were seldom called in question while he lived, and now that he has gone his memory will be held in blessed remembrance by his countrymen, and especially by that race whose shackles of slavery were broken during his administration, and who will cherish his name as that of their great Liberator.

He has conducted us safely through the checkered career of the greatest civil war known in the history of the world; and at the time of his decease his clear and honest intellect was engaged upon those great and difficult problems of statesmanship which, after such a conflict appertain to a condition of peace. At times when disaster befell our arms, or confusion attended our councils, and the timid were disposed to give up in despair,

his faith never wavered in the final success of the cause — new difficulties aroused new energies — and, relying upon the patriotism of the people, he moved on with a resolute will, in the work which Providence had placed in his hands for the salvation of the nation.

The great responsibilities of his position, he bore with complacency and good humor. His physical frame, which was developed in early manhood, fitted him for the unparalleled labors of his public trust ; and his tragic death was caused by that fell spirit of treason and disloyalty, which, had it not been for his efforts, might likewise have been the death of the nation.

The Republic has lost its chief officer ; — every patriot feels that he has lost a personal friend. We finite beings cannot fathom the wisdom of the great calamity. He that ruleth

over the nations of the earth must be our
abiding trust. To the family of the late President, our heartfelt sympathies and condolence
should be tendered.

In common with the whole nation, this community joins in the general sorrow; and in
order that you may officially take that public
notice of the event which the occasion de-
mands, I have called the members of the City
Council together in special session.

Your wisdom will suggest the most appropriate manner for the city of Boston to honor
the memory of the distinguished dead.

F. W. LINCOLN, Jr., Mayor.

At the conclusion of the Mayor's Address, Alderman GEORGE W. MESSINGER, Chairman of the
Board spoke, as follows: —

It is with no ordinary emotions, Mr. Mayor,
that I rise to offer the resolutions pertinent

to this occasion. The sudden shock which our entire community experienced at the reception of the astounding reports from Washington; the mingled feelings of grief, of horror, and of indignation, have scarcely yet subsided; the repose and reflections incident to the Sabbath may have served to calm and tranquillize, but only to bring forth a more realizing sense of the irreparable loss which the nation has sustained by the death of its Chief Magistrate.

At the very time when the rebellion appears subdued, when the days of battle are numbered and the horrors of war are to give way to the blessings of peace, when the restoration or reconstruction of our glorious Union is so evident, that great and good man, at the head of our nation, whose sound judgment and valuable counsels were so much relied on, is stricken

down by the hand of the assassin. Without further comment, I now submit the preamble and resolutions prepared by a joint committee of the City Council: —

RESOLVES.

Whereas, in the Providence of God, the shadow of a great grief is now resting on the people of the United States, in the sudden death, by the hand of violence, of their beloved and honored Chief Magistrate, ABRAHAM LINCOLN, now officially announced to the City Council by His Honor the Mayor, therefore,

Resolved, 1. That in this early hour of the Nation's bereavement and sorrow, the greatness of our loss cannot be adequately expressed by words, but is evinced by the unspoken and unutterable language of the heart, and the tears of millions of our loyal countrymen, telling how

truly and affectionately he who was from the people, and loved the people, was loved by them.

2. That we devoutly thank God for the noble work our loved and honored President was permitted to do for the nation, guiding it with consummate sagacity and skill through the most difficult epoch of its existence; that we recognize especially his great wisdom and foresight in issuing his proclamation of Emancipation, which will entitle him to the gratitude of the lovers of liberty throughout the world in all future ages, and give him a place in his country's fame by the side of the immortal WASHINGTON.

3. That we accord to the family of our late Chief Magistrate our heartfelt and tender sympathy in their irreparable loss, assuring them that we cherish as one of our country's price-

less legacies the memory of him whom the nation mourns.

4. That the atrocious attempt to take the life of our Secretary of State, the Hon. William H. Seward, and the assaults on the members of his household, have excited the liveliest interest for his preservation; and we trust that his life may long be spared, and his valuable counsels continue to benefit his country.

5. That we assure PRESIDENT JOHNSON of our cordial support in the great task devolved upon him by this horrible crime, entreating him to believe that the nation instructed by this last bitter experience, will sustain the Government more unitedly than ever in vigorous and effective measures for suppressing a wicked and unnatural rebellion, in meting out justice to all its abettors, and securing the amplest guarantees for peace in all coming time; trusting that

he will not pause until every seed of its possible life is destroyed, and our whole country rests on the sure basis of full and impartial liberty.

6. That as a proper mark of respect, Faneuil Hall and the City Hall be draped in mourning for the period of thirty days, and that on the day of the funeral ceremonies in Washington, His Honor, the Mayor order all public offices, schools and places of amusement to be closed, and request an entire suspension of business on the part of our citizens.

7. That a delegation from the city government, consisting of His Honor, Mayor Lincoln, two Aldermen, the President and three members of the Common Council, attend the obsequies of the late President of the United States.

8. That a eulogy on the character and services of ABRAHAM LINCOLN be pronounced

before the city government at an early day, and that a joint committee be appointed to make the necessary arrangements.

9. That a copy of these resolutions be sent to the President of the United States, the heads of the different departments at Washington, and the family of the deceased.

The passage of the foregoing resolutions having been advocated by Alderman Nathaniel C. Nash, with some appropriate remarks, they were unanimously adopted by the Board, each member rising in his place.

The Chair having appointed Aldermen John S. Tyler and Charles F. Dana as a Committee in behalf of this Board to attend the Funeral Obsequies in Washington, and Aldermen George W. Messinger, John S. Tyler, and Thomas Gaffield upon the Committee of Arrangement for a Eulogy on the deceased, as contemplated in the eighth resolve, said resolutions were sent down to

the Common Council for concurrence, and the Board of Aldermen then adjourned.

Attest:

S. F. McCLEARY, *City Clerk.*

PROCEEDINGS OF THE COMMON COUNCIL.

The members of the Common Council were called to order by their President, William B. Fowle, Esq., who addressed them as follows:—

GENTLEMEN OF THE COMMON COUNCIL:

Were I to consult my own feelings upon this occasion, I should indulge in speechless sorrow; but, as representatives of our fellow-citizens, it seems proper that we should place upon record our estimation of the great and good man whose loss the nation mourns.

Words are but feeble instruments to express

deep grief; far better the sympathizing grasp of the hand and the eye glistening with the involuntary tear.

We respected Abraham Lincoln as the chief magistrate of our country, and as such alone we should have felt sorrow at his death, but we are now in mourning for more than the loss of the nation's head.

Our country needed him. The marked ability with which he had steadied the helm through the long night of civil war, until the dayspring of peace seemed fairly opening to our vision, had taught us to look to him as the guiding star under whose benignant auspices all troubles were to cease. But deeper seated than even this is our grief to-day.

He was cut off by a dastardly act in the midst of such usefulness as it has rarely been the lot

of man to experience. We lament the cruel manner of his death, and our grief deepens at the thought that for us and in our service he died. But even this does not sufficiently account for the gloom which rests upon us.

Beyond the magistrate whose ability we respected, beyond the victim of the assassin, who died for us and whose untimely fate we deplore, beyond the loss of his services at a time when they were so sorely needed, we each and all of us have lost a dear friend; a great, good, honest, noble-hearted friend whom we all loved. Our *love* for him is the great cause of our heartfelt grief.

Upon our nation's roll of honor, side by side with that of the immortal Washington, let us place the name of Abraham Lincoln, and let us pray to the Supreme Ruler, that the exigencies

of our country may nevermore need that a third should be added to those two

> . . . . "immortal names,
> That were not born to die!"

The message of the Mayor having been read, the resolutions adopted by the Board of Aldermen were then submitted to the Common Council. Their passage by this branch of the City Council was advocated by Messrs. Clement Willis of Ward 8, Joseph Story of Ward 5, Benjamin Dean of Ward 12, and Solomon B. Stebbins of Ward 10, who spoke most earnestly and appropriately on the subject. The resolutions were then passed unanimously in concurrence, each member present rising in his place.

The Chair appointed Messrs. Solomon B. Stebbins of Ward 10, Benjamin Dean of Ward 12, and Moses W. Richardson of Ward 11, delegates on behalf of the Common Council to attend the funeral obsequies at Washington. And the President of the Common Council, together with Messrs. Joseph Story of Ward 5, John C. Haynes of Ward 9, Sumner Crosby of Ward 12, William D. Park of Ward 7, and Solomon B. Stebbins of

Ward 10, were joined to the Committee of Arrangements for the proposed eulogy on the illustrious deceased.

The Common Council then adjourned.

Attest: W. P. GREGG, *Clerk.*